LITTLE DOG,
BIG BORK

By: Fiza Javid

WHEN THE SUN COMES UP

ALL MIGHTY AND BRIGHT

IT PEAKS THROUGH THE WINDOW

LIKE A SHINY SPOTLIGHT...

THERE AWAKES MAX

WHERE HE YAWNS AND HE YIPS...

HE DOES HIS DOGGY STRETCHES

AND WIGGLES HIS HIPS...

H<small>E GREETS HIS SISTER</small> M<small>ILA</small>...

AND WAITS FOR THE
SOUNDS
THAT MAKE UP HIS DAY.

JINGLE! JINGLE!

WHAT WAS THAT?

THAT WAS THE
SOUND
OF THE KEYS!

MAX KNOWS EXACTLY
WHAT THAT SOUND MEANS...

Time to roll in the grass...

And play with the sticks...

After running around in circles...

He will practice his tricks...

SQUEAK! SQUEAK!
WHAT WAS THAT?

IT'S THE SOUND OF HIS
TOY...

WHEN HE PLAYS WITH
BUDDY MONKEYS...

HE FEELS NOTHING BUT

J O Y...

He loves the sound of cheering

CRUNCH!

CRUNCH!

CRUNCH!

CRUNCH!

The *CRUNCH* of his food

BUT THERE IS ONE SOUND THAT PUTS MAX IN A
VERY BAD MOOD...

HE CLIMBS TO THE WINDOW AND WAITS
HE CHECKS HIS WATCH
AND HE WAITS...

3 O' CLOCK!

There he is! Mr. Tillman, the mailman
Walking to the neighbor's home.

MAX LIFTS HIS EARS...

THEY GO LEFT...

THEY GO RIGHT...

MR. TILLMAN PICKS UP THE MAIL
REACHES OUT HIS HAND TO THE
DOORBELL

AND...

AND THROUGH ALL THE BORKS
FOR A MOMENT IN TIME
HE AWAKES THE DOGS AROUND THE WORLD

From China to Japan
to India and Ireland
From London to Greece
From the west to the east
The dogs around the world
for hundreds of miles
Jump to their windows
where they bork and they howl
They woof and they yip
They paw and they plead
The sound of the neighbor's doorbell
started a bork stampede

THE BORK GROWS BIGGER...

AND BIGGER...

BORK! BORK!
BORK! BORK! BORK!
BORK! BORK!
BORK! BORK!
BORK! BORK!
BORK! BORK!
BORK! BORK!
BORK! BORK!
BORK! BORK! BORK!
BORK! BORK! BORK!
BORK! BORK!

UNTIL...

"TIME FOR A
WALK!"

Max and Mila secure their leashes
They walk to the west
They walk to the east
They walk back home
where they enjoy a treat.

"YAAAAWWWNNN..."
MAX EXCLAIMS

YAAAAAWWWWWWN!

IT'S TIME FOR SLEEPY SLEEPIES...

AS MAX RESTS TO PREPARE FOR ANOTHER
GLORIOUS DAY.

Made in the USA
Monee, IL
12 September 2021